Ella Louise
SAVES
CHRISTMAS

Written By

Beth Slagle
Stephanie Nardello

Illustrated By

Beth Slagle

Published by Twisted V Creative, LLC
Copyright ©2019 Beth Slagle, Twisted V Creative, LLC & Stephanie Nardello, All rights reserved
ISBN 978-1-7341398-0-8
First Edition November 2019

To all the Bubbas I've known and loved and to
those I have yet to meet -
my heart is with you.

- Beth

To my Carmella (Ella) and Charlotte (Louise) -
you are my inspiration
and greatest adventure.

- Stephanie

To Craig, Chris, Shannon - Thank you for reading and listening to this story umpteen times and never once uttering the words "please stop." Your constructive criticism, at times, was painful, but your help and encouragement have been invaluable. To the numerous other people (you know who you are) who took time to edit, review and comment on this book - thank you from the bottom of our hearts. And with very special thanks to Paula Patterson who Beth didn't have as much appreciation for while in high school English class as she does now. Thank you for your encouragement, editing and continued lessons in proper English.

Allow me to introduce myself. My name is Ella Louise and I'm 7 years, 4 months, and 2 days old.

My parents say I'm inquisitive and precocious, whatever that means. I stiII have to look that up.

My brother says I'm annoying, but what does he know? He's smelly.

I know the truth. I'm a junior detective extraordinaire who solves mysteries. I go by the name E.L. when I'm on a case.

Oh, and my most favorite thing is my teddy bear, Murphy P. Fluffenopolous, The Magnificent. Friends call him Bubba.

I HAVE to tell you about my best friend Bubba. Murphy P. Fluffenpolous,
The Magnificent, is not your ordinary stuffed animal.

He is filled with magic. When we have a mission, he shakes, rattles, and rolls
until he turns into a giant, cuddly monster, and together we solve all mysteries,
great and small.

When we are in detective mode, I yell to Bubba, "IT'S GO TIME!", and we jump on my prized book, which is magical and enchanted.

It flies us wherever our mission takes us. Here, there and anywhere - any place we need to go.

My favorite adventure was the night we saved Christmas. It all started with a dog in the North Pole.

Let me tell you about it.

It was the day before Christmas at Santa's workshop. Mrs. Claus and the elves were so busy that they didn't notice Santa's best, furry friend and loyal dog, Noel, jump into a box being sent out for delivery.

Noel never missed a Christmas and always helped Santa deliver presents, but this year, she was about to become one!

Back at home, knowing that tomorrow was THE BIG DAY, I was behaving myself in case Santa was still watching when I heard a knock at the door. What looked like another boring package started wiggling. THE BOX WIGGLED. And then it barked. "ARRRFF!"

I'm not supposed to open boxes without my mom, but it BARKED and it WIGGLED! I couldn't help myself. Inside was the sweetest puppy with Noel on her name tag. My parents got me a puppy!

Sadly, Mommy and Daddy didn't get me a puppy. Noel arrived by mistake, but there was no way to return her since it was Christmas Eve.

So Noel had to spend the night. Yay!

That evening, I cuddled up with Bubba and Noel in my secret reading place and pulled out my favorite Christmas book about Santa.

On every Christmas Eve, Santa and Noel deliver presents to children around the world. Noel is Santa's top navigator and a lookout for children who are not nestled snug in their beds.

Most importantly, she helps Santa gobble up all of the scrumptious cookies families set out.

Santa and Noel

There in the book was a picture of Santa and his dog, Noel. The book said that Santa could only deliver presents on Christmas Eve if Noel was with him. Well, that's interesting, I thought, looking at Noel. My Noel and Santa's Noel looked alike. Pointing to the book, I looked at Noel and asked, "is this you?" Her loud bark sounded like "Yes!" She shook her head up and down and gave me a big, slobbery lick up the side of my face. That's when I realized, "Oh my! I have Santa's dog!" Christmas will be ruined if we don't get Noel back to the North Pole by midnight!

I knew we didn't have much time to return Noel to Santa before he had to start his journey. "It's GO TIME! We have to save Christmas!" I shouted to Bubba.

Bubba shook and rattled and made funny faces as he grew and grew.

"Jump on," I yelled, and off we flew on my magical book.

"Wheeeeee!" Bubba squealed. He loved to fly. "Wheeeeee!" he squealed again, admiring his large, purple size.

"Does my fur look fluffy enough?" he asked nervously. "I want to look perfect for Santa."

"Oh Bubba," I giggled.

We weren't even out of the neighborhood when Bubba started whining.

"Brrrrrrrrrrrrrr, I'm chilly," he sniffled. "Like really, really, really freeeeeezing."

"You're furry – how can you be so cold?" I exclaimed. "We don't have time to stop. We have to get Noel to Santa!"

"Cold, cold, cold," he muttered through rattling teeth.

We made a quick stop. Anything to keep Bubba from complaining.

Bubba sprang from the store wearing a red polka dotted scarf and Christmas mittens for his hands, ears, and tail. "Mittens for your ears and tail?" I asked, shaking my head. "They were on sale," he proudly said.

"I look pretty spiffy, don't you think? Perfect for when I see Santa!" he smiled with his big toothy grin.

"Come on! We've got to keep going!" He jumped on with a THUD, and off we flew.

Not even 10 minutes later, there was a grumbling, rumbling tummy sound.

"I need a snack," Bubba whined. "I'm really, really, really HUNNGGRRYY."

"Why didn't you get something at the store when we stopped?" I asked.

"I didn't know then that I would be hungry now," Bubba whimpered.

And his tummy rumbled, grumbled, growled, and roared. It was so loud I couldn't hear myself think.

One last stop. Bubba promised it would be the last.

"Thanks, E.L.!" Bubba said, happily stuffing himself with pizza and chips.

I guess this stop wasn't so bad - it was pizza after all. And off we flew again.

"Are we there yet??" Bubba whined.

"Oh Bubba," I sighed. I didn't say it out loud, but I was thinking the same thing. I don't think any of us realized how far the North Pole was.

Well, except for Noel, of course.

We were so excited to finally arrive at Santa's workshop until we saw the sign on the gates saying "CLOSED - Searching for Noel."

It was only a few minutes before Santa had to start his journey at midnight. If we can't get Noel to Santa in time, Christmas would be canceled! Oh no!

CLOSED
—
SEARCHING
FOR NOEL

As we stood at the locked gates, everyone else in the North Pole – animals, humans, and elves - searched for Noel.

"How can we get Noel to Santa? The gates are locked! We can't climb over. It's so very high. And they're too narrow to squeeze through."

"I think I have something to help!" Bubba excitedly said. And with that, he whipped out a pogo stick.

"Where in the world did you get that?" I shrieked.

"From my pocket," he squealed. "I always wanted one, and I saw it in the window. What a great deal!" He was pretty proud of himself.

I realized, then, that one of our stops along the way very well could have saved Christmas.

After several attempts, we weren't giving up.
We took one giant jump and up, up and OVER
we sailed!!!

I was a little nervous, but Noel and Bubba laughed
with glee as we bounced so, so high.

As soon as we landed, we ran as fast as we could to Santa's workshop.

"Ella Louise! You saved Christmas!" Santa exclaimed, giving me a giant squeeze - the best hug I ever got.

While Santa and Mrs. Claus asked in wonder about our adventure, Bubba nervously checked to see whether he had made the nice list this year.

"And don't worry, Murphy P. Fluffenpolous, The Magnificent. You are DEFINITELY on the nice list," Santa said while laughing.

We left Santa's workshop, relieved that Noel was with Santa, and they could start their journey. It was now time for me and Bubba to go home.

"Bubba, is that what I think it was?" I sighed.

"Ummmm . . . E.L. I have to go to the potty."

"BUBBA, I TOLD YOU TO GO BEFORE WE LEFT!"

It was going to be a long flight home.

We arrived safely and snuggled in my bed. "Love you E.L." Bubba slee
"Love you too, Bubba," and I hugged him a little tighter.

This was the best night ever I thought, happily knowing that Christmas was saved.

As I drifted off to sleep, I was sure I could hear Santa's jolly laugh and Noel's happy bark wishing all a Merry Christmas.